For my family, who are the best caregivers I know

—R. R.

For my mom

—C. S.

BLOOMSBURY CHILDREN'S BOOKS
Bloomsbury Publishing Inc., part of Bloomsbury Publishing Plc
1385 Broadway, New York, NY 10018

BLOOMSBURY, BLOOMSBURY CHILDREN'S BOOKS, and the Diana logo are trademarks of Bloomsbury Publishing Plc

First published in the United States of America in February 2019 by Bloomsbury Children's Books

Bloomsbury books may be purchased for business or promotional use. For information on bulk purchases please contact Macmillan Corporate and Premium Sales Department at
specialmarkets@macmillan.com

Library of Congress Cataloging-in-Publication Data
Names: Roan, Rebecca, author. | Santoso, Charles, illustrator.
Title: Dragons get colds too / by Rebecca Roan ; illustrated by Charles Santoso.
Description: New York : Bloomsbury, 2019.
Summary: A guidebook to caring for one's sick dragon, full of facts and tips for medicating, feeding, entertaining, and helping the dragon get the rest it needs.
Identifiers: LCCN 2018026064 (print) | LCCN 2018031577 (e-book)
ISBN 978-1-68119-044-0 (hardcover)
ISBN 978-1-68119-973-3 (e-book) • ISBN 978-1-68119-974-0 (e-PDF)
Subjects: | CYAC: Dragons—Fiction. | Medical care—Fiction. |
Cold (Disease)—Fiction. | Humorous stories.
Classification: LCC PZ7.1.R5777 Dr 2109 (print) | LCC PZ7.1.R5777 (e-book) | DDC [E]—dc23
LC record available at https://lccn.loc.gov/2018026064

Art created digitally
Typeset in Billy; hand lettering by Charles Santoso
Book design by Heather Palisi
Printed in China by Leo Paper Products, Heshan, Guangdong
2 4 6 8 10 9 7 5 3 1

All papers used by Bloomsbury Publishing Plc are natural, recyclable products made from wood grown in well-managed forests.
The manufacturing processes conform to the environmental regulations of the country of origin.

To find out more about our authors and books visit www.bloomsbury.com
and sign up for our newsletters.

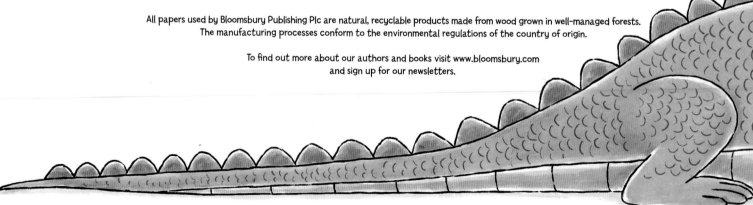

DRAGONS GET COLDS TOO

Rebecca Roan

illustrated by Charles Santoso

BLOOMSBURY
CHILDREN'S BOOKS

NEW YORK   LONDON   OXFORD   NEW DELHI   SYDNEY

Every new dragon owner learns that just like humans, dragons get colds too. However, caring for a sick dragon can be a daunting task.

Follow these simple steps, and your dragon is sure to feel better in no time at all!

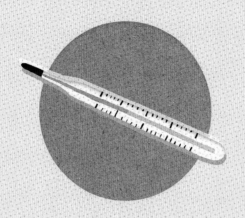

STEP 1

Determine that your dragon
does indeed have a cold.

FACT Dragons rarely use tissues due to their flammability. Instead, dragons try to wipe their noses on acceptable alternatives.

TIP A dragon seldom wears sleeves, so your sleeve is the next best thing. For sanitary reasons, keep extra shirts handy. Dragon snot tends to be rather gooey.

Thanks to your skillful investigation, it's official:
you have a sick dragon. It's time for treatment.

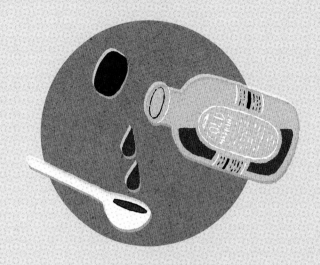

STEP 2

Give your dragon the proper cold medicine. (Please contact your local dragon pharmacy for more information.)

FACT It is nearly impossible to give medicine to dragons.

TIP The classic spoon-airplane method is a simple and effective distraction technique. Yet, your dragon may require a bit more creativity. It's best to have a full dance routine ready. But remember, dragons are rather harsh critics.

Now that you have medicated your dragon,
it is important to feed it an adequately
nutritious meal.

STEP 3

Feed your dragon spicy food. It is the perfect thing to clear out that stuffy nose!

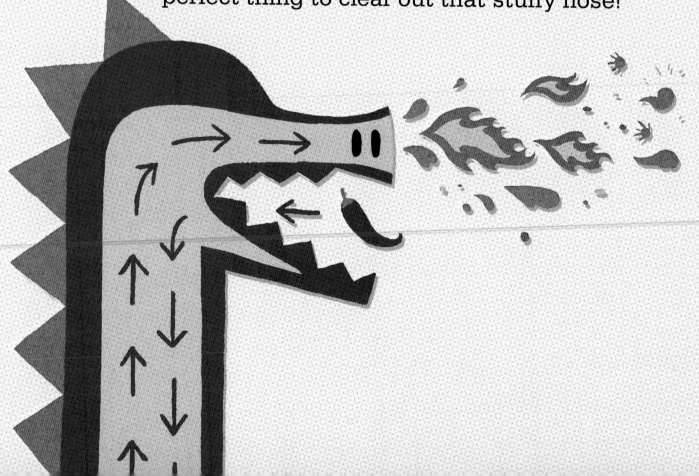

FACT Dragons love volcanic sushi rolls and exploding chili rice cakes.

TIP Wear protective clothing if following this step. Fiery sneezes and rotten, fishy burps could prove dangerous, so proceed with extreme caution.

Excellent work. Your dragon's tummy is now satisfied. Next, your dragon is probably looking for something fun to do.

STEP 4

Entertain your dragon.

FACT Bored dragons are grumpy dragons, especially when they are stuck inside.

TIP Choose activities that will appeal to your dragon. Try a board game or a charming giraffe puzzle. Dragons think giraffes, with their long necks and skinny legs, are hilarious. One giraffe puzzle guarantees at least one hour of uninterrupted dragon amusement.

Great! Your dragon is now sufficiently entertained. Although all the fun is most likely wearing it out.

STEP 5

Sick dragons need lots of rest.

FACT Dragons absolutely hate to rest.

TIP If your dragon is being especially stubborn, offer to read it a book. Consider building a fort for the two of you to read in. And always bring flashlights. Shadow puppets in a fort are a must. Everyone knows this.

Fantastic! You have eased your
dragon into a restful slumber.
Now, make sure to keep it that way.

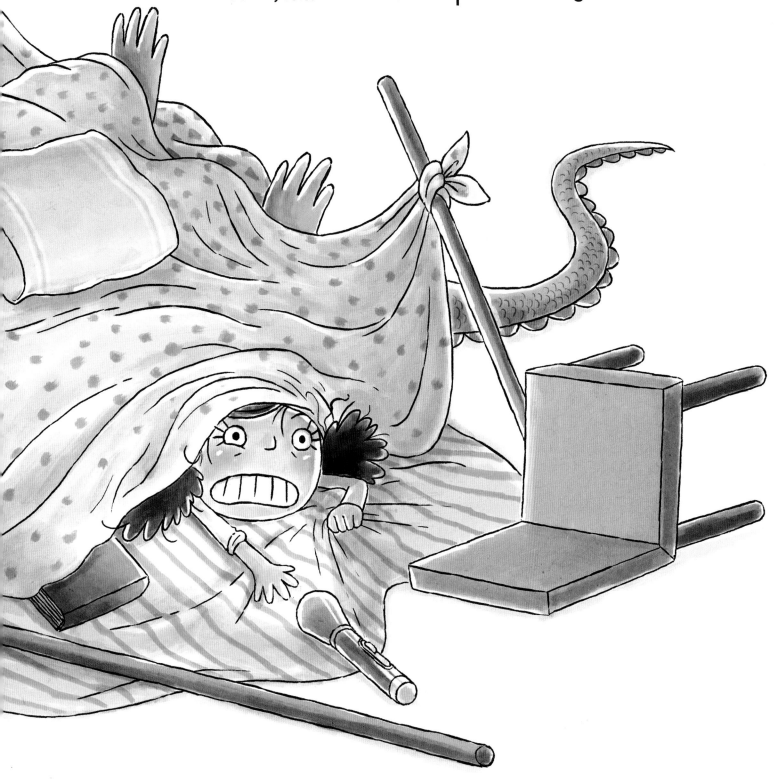

STEP 6

Never wake a sleeping dragon.

FACT Sick dragons tend to fall asleep anywhere and everywhere.

TIP Leave your dragon wherever it has fallen asleep, and do your best to avoid any noisy activities while it slumbers. Don't be fooled by those deep snores though. Dragons are very light sleepers.

Outstanding! Your dragon is getting the rest it needs. Here comes the final step.

STEP 7

Dragons need time to recover.

FACT Dragons on the mend are terrible at remembering to take it easy.

TIP Singing along to some favorite tunes is the perfect activity for any music-loving dragon. Consider adding an instrument of your own making to the mix. Except don't forget to wear earplugs. Dragons are enthusiastic but extremely tone-deaf.

Congratulations! You have successfully nursed your sick dragon back to health. You see, with a little confidence and guidance, anyone can tackle the challenge of caring for their dragon.

And remember, if you take good care of your dragon, your dragon will always take good care of you!

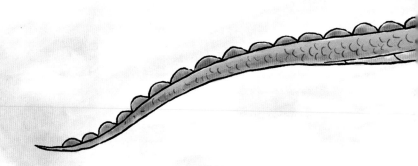